THE LUCKY
BASEBALL BAT

With Illustrations by

ROBERT HENNEBERGER

THE LUCKY
BASEBALL
BAT

by Matt Christopher

Little, Brown and Company

New York   Boston   London

To
Marty, Pam, and Dale

Copyright © 1954 by Matt Christopher Royalties, Inc.

Little, Brown and Company

Hachette Book Group
237 Park Avenue, New York, NY 10017
Visit our website at lb-kids.com

mattchristopher.com

Little, Brown and Company is a division of Hachette Book Group, Inc.
The Little, Brown name and logo are trademarks of Hachette Book Group, Inc.

The publisher is not responsible for websites (or their content) that are not owned by the publisher.

First Anniversary Edition: August 2004
First published in hardcover in 1954 by Little, Brown and Company

Matt Christopher® is a registered trademark of Matt Christopher Royalties, Inc.

Library of Congress Control Number: 54-5141

ISBN: 978-0-316-01012-2

20 19 18 17 16 15 14 13

CWO

Printed in the United States of America

THE LUCKY
BASEBALL BAT

I

MARVIN bit his lip and mopped his damp forehead with a grimy handkerchief. His sister Jeannie, two years younger than he, scowled at him.

"What're you afraid of? Go in there and ask them."

"Ask who?" Marvin said.

He looked from her to the group of boys scattered on the ball field. They were practicing, just throwing the ball among themselves to limber up their

3

muscles and get the feel of it. The sun was shining through a thin layer of cloud, with a lot of blue sky around it. Many of the boys wore short-sleeved jerseys.

Jeannie brushed a tangle of curly hair away from her eyes and pointed. "Ask that man there. Jim Cassell. He's the captain or something, isn't he?"

Marvin didn't like to go and ask Jim Cassell. Jim might tell him to go home. He didn't know Marvin, and Marvin didn't know him. That was the trouble. Marvin hardly knew anybody here. They had just moved into the city.

"I think I'll just go out there with those kids and see if they'll throw a ball to me," he said after thinking for a

while. "That'll be all right, won't it?"

Jeannie nodded. "Go ahead. Maybe it's the best way, anyway."

Marvin felt pleased because he had figured that one out without anybody's help. He started out at a slow run toward the scattered group of boys. They were all about his size, some a little smaller, some taller. Most of them had baseball gloves. He wished he had one. You didn't look like a baseball player without a baseball glove.

All at once he heard Jim Cassell's voice shout out to them. "Okay, boys! Spread out! A couple of you get in center field!"

The boys scampered into position. Marvin didn't move. Jim Cassell was

6

having the boys start batting practice. A tall, skinny kid stood on the mound. He pitched the ball twice. Each time the boy at bat swung at the ball and missed.

The third time he connected. Marvin heard the sharp crack! It was followed by a scramble of feet not far behind him. He looked up and sure enough the ball, like a small white pill, was curving through the air in his direction!

"I got it! I got it!" he cried. He forgot that he had no glove. His sneakers slipped on the short-cut grass as he tried to get in position under the ball.

Somebody bumped into him, but he didn't give ground. "I got it!" he yelled again.

The ball came directly at him and he reached for it with both hands. The next instant it changed to a blur and he felt it slide through his hands and strike solidly against his chest.

His heart sank. Missed it!

"Nice catch!" a boy sneered. "Where did you learn how to play ball?"

Marvin gave him a cold look and shut his lips tight to keep his anger from spilling out. Another boy who had come running over stopped and threw darts with his eyes too.

"Who do you think you are, trying to catch a ball without a glove? Next time leave it alone," he said.

Marvin looked at his bare hands, feeling his heart pound in his chest. He walked away, sticking his hands into his pockets. He could feel the hot sun burning his neck.

"Kid!" Jim Cassell's voice yelled from across the field. "Hey, son!"

Marvin turned.

"For Petey sakes," Jim said, "don't try to catch a ball without a glove! You'll get hurt!"

Marvin looked away, his lips still pressed tight together. "Come on," he said to Jeannie. "Let's go home."

"Sure," Jeannie replied in disgust. "You can do something else besides play baseball with those boys."

"But I don't want to do anything else!" Marvin said, angrily. "I want to play baseball!"

9

Then he looked up. A tall, dark-haired boy was watching him — a boy of high-school size, with broad shoulders. He seemed to be amused about something.

2

"HELLO," said the high-school boy. "What's the matter, fella? You look as if you'd lost your best friend!"

Marvin tried to smile, just to show that he wasn't mad at everybody. "Nothing's the matter," he answered, his eyes on the ground. He kept walking with his hands in his pockets, his heels scraping the dirt and pebbles. Jeannie had hold of his arm, as if whatever suffering he was going through she was going through with him.

"Hey, wait a minute!" the tall stranger called after them as they started by. He caught Marvin's arm in his big fist and Marvin had to stop. The smile on the stranger's face turned into a bigger one. "You didn't answer me. What happened? Won't they let you play ball with them?"

"I haven't got a glove," Marvin said. "I'm sure I could catch those balls if I had a glove."

The tall boy laughed. Marvin liked the sound and turned to look at Jeannie to see what she was thinking. Her blue eyes were crinkling in a cheerful grin, and Marvin knew she felt the same way he did. Whoever this tall boy was, he was nice.

"Tell you what," the stranger said. "My name's Barry Welton. I live about two blocks around the corner on Grant Street, to the right."

"We live a block to the left," Jeannie said warmly. "I'm Jeannie Allan, and this is my brother Marvin."

"Well! That's fine!" He made a motion with his hand. "Come on," he said, and began to walk toward Grant Street.

"Where you going?" Marvin asked, wondering.

"To my house. I'm going to give you something. Something I think you'll like to have."

When they reached his house, a gray wooden frame building with yellow shutters, he asked them to wait in the living room while he ran upstairs. He came back down a couple of seconds later, and Marvin's eyes almost bugged from his head.

Barry was carrying a bat and a glove!

"Here," he grinned. "These are yours. Now maybe they'll let you play. Okay?"

"Christmas!" Marvin cried. "You mean you're giving these things to me?"

"Certainly! I've had that glove ever since I was your size, and I outgrew that bat years ago. It was a lucky bat for me. Maybe it'll be a lucky one for you, too."

"Christmas!" said Marvin again, his heart thumping excitedly. "Thanks! Thanks a lot, Barry!"

He could not make up his mind whether to return to the ball diamond or not. Those boys had not liked it because he had butted in on them by trying to catch a ball without a glove. But he had a glove now. They shouldn't say anything.

"Come on, Jeannie. Let's go back to the park," he said.

She looked at him strangely, then together they walked back to the ball field.

Marvin saw that they were still having batting practice. He let Jeannie hang on to the bat while he put on the glove and ran out to the field. Two of the boys saw him with his glove, and said something to each other. He acted as if he didn't see them. He didn't care what they said. He had as much right here as the rest of them.

Suddenly he saw Jim Cassell gazing toward the outfield. Jim seemed to be looking directly at him, and Marvin's heart fell.

"Kid!" Jim yelled then, motioning with his hand. "Move over a little — toward center field!"

A thrill of excitement went through him. Jim Cassell had given him an order as if he were already a member of the team!

He ran over to a spot between left and center fields. He almost prayed a ball would come his way. He had not caught a ball since last summer, but he knew how to do it. Maybe he could even show them something!

And then, even while he was thinking about it, he saw a ball hit out his way. The closer of the two boys Jim Cassell had placed in center field came running for it, shouting at the top of his lungs, "I've got it! I've got it!"

Marvin knew it was his ball more than the other boy's. He needed only to take four or five steps backward. He reached up, trying to make his yell sound out above the other's.

"It's mine! Let it go! It's mine!"

"Let him take it, Tommy!" Jim Cassell's voice boomed from near home plate.

Marvin felt a shoulder hit his arm. It threw him off balance enough so that the ball struck the fingers of his glove and slipped right through. Bang! On his chest again, barely missing his throat. The ball dropped to the grass and bounced away.

Marvin turned, tears choking him. It was the same boy who had earlier made a nasty remark to him.

"So it's you again," the boy said. "With a glove, too!" He laughed. "Even with a glove you miss them. Why don't you go home and stay there? We don't want any farmers on this team!"

3

THIS time when Marvin and Jeannie went home there was no Barry Welton around. Marvin was glad Barry had not seen how foolish he looked on the diamond.

"I'm glad you came home, children," their mother said, as she saw them coming through the hall into the kitchen. "We're almost ready for supper."

Then she caught sight of the bat and

20

glove Marvin was carrying. Her mouth made an oval. "Where on earth did you get those things?" she cried.

"A big boy by the name of Barry Welton gave them to me," Marvin said, and told his mother what had happened. She seemed surprised, but quite happy about Barry Welton's gift to Marvin.

The cellar door opened and Marvin's tall, husky father came in and stared at the bat and glove, too. Marvin had to tell all about it again. He left out one thing, though. He didn't tell them he was going to give the bat and glove back to Barry.

He did not feel like eating much for supper, but once he started his appetite improved. He had another helping and almost finished it before he caught his mother looking at him strangely. He slowed up but it was too late.

"Marvin, what's your hurry?"

"I'm sorry, Mother," he said. He didn't want to tell her he had baseball on his mind.

Marvin went outside after supper, and sat on the front porch in the shade. He expected Jeannie as soon as she finished helping Mother with the dishes. For a minute he got to thinking about Jeannie. If she had been a boy everything would have been all right. They could play baseball together, and get a lot of practice, and chum around like real pals. You can't do those things with a sister, he thought, even though Jeannie tried to be like a boy with him.

He didn't know how long he sat out there thinking. But all at once he heard leather heels clicking on the sidewalk. They were coming from down the street, and even before he looked to see who was making the sound, he knew who it was. It was Barry Welton.

"Hi, Barry!" he greeted when Barry got closer. It was hard to smile.

"Hi, Marv," Barry answered. "Taking it easy?"

Marvin nodded. "Wait a minute, Barry," he said, and went into the house. "I'll be right back."

He got the bat and glove and brought them out. "Here," he said, swallowing a lump in his throat. "Take them back,

Barry. They'll never let me play base-ball around here!"

Barry frowned, then a grin came over his face. "Shucks, now, pal. Don't go acting like that or you'll never play ball! Have you got a ball?"

"In the house," Marvin said, wondering what Barry was driving at.

"Get it. We'll play a little catch."

Marvin ran into the house, full of excitement. The ball was in the closet where he kept all his things. He brought it out and tossed it to Barry.

"Let's go out to the side of the house," Barry said, "so that we won't be throwing toward the windows. You get over there and I'll have my back toward the street. Just make sure you

don't throw any wide balls!" he
laughed.

"I'll try not to," Marvin said, and
they started throwing the ball back and

forth between them, Marvin using the glove, and Barry barehanded. Marvin thrilled at the expert way Barry was catching the balls, pulling his hands down and away with the ball. He tried to do the same. Only, with the glove, he didn't have to do it so much.

They played about fifteen minutes, then Barry said he had to move along. He'd see Marvin tomorrow. In the meantime Jeannie had come out to sit on the porch, watching them. After Barry left, Marvin still wanted to play.

"Jeannie," he said, "how about throwing the ball to me in the back yard? I'll bat. Then after a while you can bat."

"Okay!"

He knew she would be willing. She was a swell sister, even if she wasn't a boy!

Out in the back yard they had much more room. The lawn was bordered by a hedge on two sides. In the back two tall elms with branches spreading out like big, crooked arms would be some protection if a ball were hit that far.

But it was not as much fun as Marvin had hoped. Each time Jeannie threw the ball he swung, and missed. He didn't want to swing too hard, of course. He might hit it squarely, and send it beyond the trees into the neighbor's yard. He might even break a window. And that he couldn't risk.

So he swung only lightly. A couple

of times he ticked the ball, and in the beginning he joked with Jeannie.

"Quit throwing those curves!" he'd say.

She would laugh, knowing as well as he that she did not have the faintest idea how to throw a curve.

But then missing the ball four, five, six times in a row got under his skin. Sweat began to break out on his forehead. He was growing warm all over, and he knew it was because he was getting anxious and mad.

"Marvin," said Jeannie, "what's the matter? Can't you even hit it?"

He took one final, hard swing. If he had hit it, it would surely have sailed beyond the big elm trees. But he missed.

28

His bat swished through the air, almost making him lose his balance.

Angrily, he threw the bat to the ground, ran around to the porch, and into the house. He ran to his bedroom, fell on his bed, and no longer tried to stop the tears.

4

MARVIN heard the door open. He didn't look up. His face was buried in the pillow. He could feel and taste the salty wetness that had soaked into it. The door closed and he heard Jeannie's voice.

"Marv, don't cry."

He didn't say anything. But hearing Jeannie made him want to stop crying.

He felt her warm hand on his back, rubbing him gently. "Please, Marv. I don't like to hear you cry. If — if you keep on, I — I'll probably start crying, too."

He rolled over on his side and wiped the tears from his cheeks with his wrist. He hated to cry. He was big now. He was ashamed to be letting tears spill all over the place. He got up.

"You're nice, Jeannie," he murmured softly.

Jeannie smiled, and he thought she really was going to cry, too.

Then a voice called from the kitchen: "Jeannie! Marvin!"

They ran out to the kitchen. Their mother was in front of the mirror, brushing her hair with short, pulling strokes. She smiled at them, her brown eyes sparkling.

"Want to go to the movies?" she asked.

"Yes!" They said it almost together, their faces brightening up like Christmas-tree bulbs.

"Well," she said, "wash yourselves and get dressed!"

They washed and put on their best going-out clothes, while their daddy went to get the car from the garage. By the time they were ready he had the car at the curb, a new-looking, pea-green sedan. They all piled in and headed for the movie. Jeannie and Marvin sat in the back seat. They were both very happy, and not once did Marvin think about baseball.

The movie was a comedy. They

laughed all the way through it.

Then they talked about it on the way home. Marvin and Jeannie told and re-told some of the funniest scenes and laughed about them. It was what they did every time after they saw a movie.

After they were home and in the house awhile Marvin remembered the bat he had left outside. Quickly, he raced out the side door, onto the porch and down the steps to the back yard. The sun had gone down, but the half-moon that hung in the sky looked big and yellow, almost close enough to hang a hat on. It made the trees and the roofs of the houses stand out sharp and black. It helped him see whatever was on the ground.

Marvin searched in and around the spot where he was sure he had left the bat. But it was nowhere around.

The bat was gone!

5

MARVIN could not sleep half the night, thinking about the bat. He thought over and over again how he had missed Jeannie's pitch, gotten mad, and thrown down the bat. That was a foolish thing to do — he knew that now. He should not have gotten mad in the first place. He should not have thrown the bat aside like that. At least, he should have gone back out right away and brought it into the house.

He would not have minded so much if Barry Welton had not given him the bat. But Barry had — and now it was gone. Somebody must have stolen it. Baseball bats don't just walk away.

Finally he fell asleep. He dreamed about the movie. He was one of the actors. He saw that another actor had the bat. But when he went to ask for it the actor showed him empty hands.

The next morning after breakfast he went out to the back yard again, just to see if he might have missed the bat last night. It could have rolled behind one of Mother's rose bushes, or into the higher grass that grew close to the wire fence. But he did not find it. The bat had really disappeared.

He walked out front. The sun, shining over the rooftops, felt hot against his face. He thought about going to the park. Maybe it was too early. Maybe none of the boys would be down there yet. He could not get the thought of the bat out of his mind. What could have happened to it? Did somebody take it? But who? And how?

He walked up to the corner where Ferrin Street crossed Grant. Down the street he saw some boys playing with a tennis ball. He recognized one of them. It was Rick Savora, who lived in the brick tenement house. The porch of the tenement house sagged on one corner and some of its windows were cracked.

Rick was about eleven or twelve —
bigger than Marvin. He stood with his
legs spread apart and held a bat on his
shoulder, waiting for another boy to
pitch him the tennis ball. Way back was
another boy, waiting to chase the ball
in case Rick hit it.

Marvin stood on the corner and
waited to see what Rick would do.
Rick, he remembered, was one of the
boys at the park yesterday. He looked
as if he might be the best player of
them all.

Suddenly Rick swung at the ball, hit
it, and it went bounding down the street
past the pitcher. Rick dropped the bat
and started scooting around squares of
cardboard which were used for bases.

Then Marvin noticed the bat. It had rolled a little way as Rick had thrown it, and then stopped. Marvin's heart pounded like mad. He started to walk down the street.

One of the boys saw him.

"Here comes that Allan kid!" he cried out.

Rick stood on second, his hands on his knees as if he were getting ready to run for third. When he heard the boy shout he rose and scowled at Marvin.

"What do you want around here?" he yelled.

Marvin didn't answer. He looked at Rick and then again at the bat. The more he looked at it the more it looked like the one Barry had given him.

The boys muttered in low tones
among themselves. One of them walked
off the street. Rick picked up the card-

board piece that was second base, tucked it under his arm, then picked up the bat. He walked off the street, too. The boy who played catcher followed him.

All three gave Marvin dirty looks and went up on the porch of the house, the boards squeaking under their weight.

Marvin stopped and watched them. A hurt look crept into his eyes and an ache filled his throat, wanting to turn into tears. He spun on his heel and headed for home. He walked a little way, then started running. For some reason he could not explain, he wanted to get away from there as fast as he could.

6

HE met Jeannie in front of the house, bouncing a rubber ball up and down on the sidewalk. She caught the ball and looked up at him in surprise.

"I was looking for you," she said.

"Rick Savora's got my bat!" Marvin exclaimed. "I just saw him take it into the house."

Jeannie's eyes widened. "Did you ask him for it?"

"No. I didn't have a chance. He and some other kids went into his house when they saw me coming down the street."

Jeannie's lips tightened. She made a face, and Marvin knew she was disgusted.

"Let's go to his house and ask him for that bat," she said.

"Suppose he won't give it to me?" Marvin asked.

"Then we'll tell Daddy about it."

Marvin shook his head. "No. I won't tell Daddy anything. I don't want him mixed up in this."

"Well, let's go anyway. If it's your bat he must have stolen it, and he must give it back. I don't like stealers."

Together they walked to Rick Savora's house. The wooden steps creaked as they climbed to the porch. Marvin knocked on the door.

A lady opened it. "Yes?" she said. She brushed a lock of dark hair away from her face, and looked curiously from Jeannie to Marvin.

"Is Rick here?" Marvin asked nervously.

"Just a minute," she said. She turned around and in a louder voice called, "Rick! Somebody to see you!"

In a minute Rick came to the door.

He scowled when he saw who his callers were.

Marvin swallowed. "You were playing with my baseball bat," he said. "I want it back."

"You're crazy!" Rick snapped. "I haven't got your bat!"

"Yes, you have. You were playing with it on the street just a little while ago. I saw it."

Rick's eyes blazed with anger, but Marvin didn't care. Rick had his bat and he wanted it back.

"Just a minute," Rick said. "I'll be right back!"

He turned away from the door. Marvin could hear his heavy footsteps as

he walked back through the house.
Pretty soon Rick returned. He had a
small yellow bat with him.

"There! Is that your bat?"

Marvin looked at it closely. "No,"

he said. "But that isn't the one you were playing with."

"You're crazy!" Rick said again. "You must've been seeing things!"

He closed the door so hard the wood panels shook. Jeannie and Marvin turned and stared at each other. Neither one knew what to say, or what to do.

"Let's go home," Marvin said then. His voice was so weak he could hardly hear it himself. He led the way down the steps.

"He's lying," he said to Jeannie as they started up the street. His heart pounded hard now. "I know he's lying!"

7

IT was a little after dinnertime when a black car stopped in front of Marvin as he sat on the porch. The man in the car said, "Hey, sonny! Want to come to the park and play ball?"

Marvin recognized Jim Cassell, manager of the small boys' team. He got off the porch and walked slowly toward the car.

Then he saw that Jim had somebody with him. Rick Savora. Rick didn't look at him.

Marvin felt a tightening in his chest. "I — I don't think so," he said. "I don't think I want to play baseball."

"Why not?" Jim Cassell's blue eyes studied Marvin, as if he could not understand why any boy did not care to play baseball.

Marvin shrugged. He did not want to say that he didn't care to play because Rick was on the team. He could not tell Jim that Rick had stolen his bat, that Rick had lied when he said he had not stolen it. It would be pretty cheap to tell on Rick. Let Jim find out himself what kind of kid Rick was. He would find out soon enough. Maybe by then Marvin would have his bat back.

Jim flashed a smile. "Got a glove?"

Marvin nodded. "Yes."

"Get it. We're going to have a team in the Grasshoppers League, and since you're one of the boys in the neighborhood maybe we'll have room for you on the team. Rick told me about you yesterday."

Marvin looked at Rick, but still Rick

did not look at him. He turned again to Jim Cassell.

"A Grasshoppers League?" He frowned. "What's that?"

"A league we have here. There are six teams in it. Each team plays two games a week during the summer vacation. The winner gets a free banquet and goes to see a World Series game. It's something worth shooting for. Don't you think so?"

"Christmas!" Marvin's face brightened. "I'll say it is!"

Jim's smile broadened. "Now you want to come along?"

"You bet! Wait! I'll run in and get my glove!"

8

AT the field Jim Cassell had two of the tallest boys choose sides. Rick Savora chose for one side, and a red-haired boy named Lennie Moore chose for the other. Marvin was picked on Lennie's team. Then Jim Cassell flipped a nickel to see whose side would bat first. Rick guessed "Heads," and chose to bat last.

Jim Cassell told the boys what positions they were to play, then called off the hitters for Lennie's team. Marvin noticed that Rick was playing short-stop. He wondered what position Jim would let him play. He had never thought about playing in a league! And to have a chance to see a World Series game! What a wonderful thing that would be! Even Daddy had never seen a World Series game!

"Okay, Marvin! Your turn to bat!"

He sprang from the bench on which he was sitting with the rest of the boys, surprised that his name was called so soon. The second one!

He picked up one of the bats and went to the plate. His heart hammered. He got into position beside the plate, tapped it a couple of times with the bat,

and waited for the pitcher to throw. The pitcher wound up once, twice, then raised his left foot and brought his throwing arm around. The next thing Marvin saw was the ball coming at him and the plate.

He swung. Missed!

Jim Cassell was umpire. "Strike!" he said. Then, "Get a little closer to the plate, Marvin. You're too far from it. And keep your feet farther apart."

He tried to do what Jim said. Again he waited for the pitch. He swung! Missed again!

Sweat came on his forehead. He was growing more nervous by the second. If he didn't hit they would see he wasn't any good. And nobody wanted a ball-player who wasn't good.

The third pitch came in. He watched it closely. He had to hit it now. He was thinking that if he had his own bat, the one Barry had given him, it would have been a cinch. This bat was too heavy.

But it was too late to think of that now.

The ball was here. Straight as an arrow. Chest-high. He swung!

He heard the ball hit into the catcher's glove. The bat carried him almost all the way around.

"Strike three!" said Jim Cassell.

9

BARRY came up the street the next morning wearing a white tee shirt with a large yellow T sewed on the front of it. Marvin wondered what the T stood for.

"Hello, Marv," Barry grinned. "You're just the fellow I want to see."

Marvin's eyes widened. "Me? What do you want to see me for, Barry?"

He wanted to ask Barry about the T, but waited to see what Barry had on his mind.

"We've got a ball game tonight with Attlee Merchants," Barry explained. "If you and your sister and your folks would like to go see it, I can get you tickets."

Marvin's face broke in a big smile. "Gee, Barry! I'd sure like to see the game! Could you wait a minute? I'll run in and ask Mother if we can go!"

Barry smiled. "Sure. Go ahead."

Marvin started to dash away, then remembered. "Barry, what does the T stand for?"

"Taunton," Barry replied.

"Thanks!" Marvin said, then tore away in a run for the big screen door. He darted inside to where his mother was ironing shirts for his father. She looked around at him.

"Well!" she exclaimed. "What are you so excited about?"

"Barry's out there," Marvin said breathlessly. "He said he can get us all tickets to his ball game if we want to go. We can go, can't we, Mother? Please?"

She smiled. "We'll have to wait to see what Daddy says. He won't be home till tonight."

His heart sank. "But he'll go, Mother. I'm sure he will. Daddy loves ball games, too!"

She rested the hot iron on the board and put an arm around him tenderly, pressing him to her. "Yes, he does, honey. I think it will be all right. Go out there and tell Barry we'll go."

"Oh, Mother!" Marvin cried, squeezing her. "You're swell!"

They sat in the grandstand, amid the fans of both teams. The evening was warm, with soft, cottony clouds drifting lazily through the sky, hiding the sun for a minute, showing it again the next. But it was shady and cool in the grandstand. Marvin, Jeannie, and their mother and father were sitting together. Marvin could hardly wait for the game to begin.

Finally the umpire cleared the field of the players who were practicing, announced the batteries, and yelled: "Play ball!"

The Taunton players ran out onto the field. Marvin saw Barry run to first base. He thought he would like to play first base too, on his team. Barry looked nice in his white baseball uniform. *Taunton* was printed on the front of his shirt in blue letters, and on his cap was a T.

Marvin sat straight, on the edge of his seat. This was sure going to be a game to watch!

The first player hit a ground ball to third. The third baseman picked it up

and threw it to Barry. Barry had to stretch way out to snare the ball in order to beat the runner.

"Out!" yelled the umpire, jerking up the thumb of his right hand.

Marvin and Jeannie clapped and yelled with the rest of the Taunton rooters. Finally there were three outs.

Attlee went out to the field and Taunton came to bat.

"Now watch Taunton!" Marvin exclaimed. "Watch Barry get a hit!"

Taunton's first two men grounded out. Marvin's hopes fell. But, he thought, just wait till Barry comes to bat. The third batter walked. When Marvin saw Barry step to the plate swinging two bats, he clapped his hands till they stung. Barry tossed one of the bats back and got in position at the plate.

"Now watch this, Jeannie!" Marvin cried. "Barry will show them how to do it!"

The first pitch was a strike. Barry didn't swing at it. The next was a ball.

Then a strike again. Barry swung and missed.

"Come on, Barry!" Marvin cried loudly. "Hit it! Hit it!"

The pitcher wound up and threw again. Barry swung with all his might. The ball made a loud *plop* in the catcher's glove.

"Strike three!" boomed the umpire. Barry had struck out!

"Oh!" Jeannie sighed.

"Don't worry," Daddy said. "He'll be up again. They can't hit the ball every time."

The innings kept piling up. Finally it was the eighth. The score was tied 1 to 1 and Taunton had one man on second. Barry came to bat. Marvin watched eagerly. So far nobody on either team had done much. It had been a pitchers' battle.

There was the pitch. Barry swung. A hit! Right over the shortstop's head! The runner on second rounded third, ran for home, and scored!

Jeannie and Marvin jumped up and down and yelled till they were hoarse.

The game ended 2 to 1.

"Goes to show," Daddy said in the car as they drove home. "Striking out didn't discourage Barry. You see, he came back and won the ball game, didn't he?"

"You bet!" exclaimed Marvin happily.

10

THE first game in the Grasshoppers League got under way at
last. Marvin's team, the Tigers, was
playing the Indians. Jim Cassell put
Marvin out in left field because Marvin
was good at catching fly balls, he said.

The Tigers had first raps. When Jim
called off the names of the first three
hitters, Marvin was never so surprised
in his life as he was to hear his name

called off second. He could not understand that, because in every practice he had been hardly able to hit the ball.

Kenny Stokes was first batter. He hit the second pitched ball for a blooping fly to the shortstop. Then Marvin walked to the plate. He wished he had his own bat. He was sure that with his own bat he would hit. It was just perfect for him. He could not find one here that fitted him. As he stood at the plate he felt a shiver go through him. Mother and Daddy were somewhere on the side lines, watching him. He wished they had not come. He didn't want them to see that he could not hit.

The pitcher threw the ball and he

wasn't ready for it. He let it go by. The umpire yelled, "Strike!"

"Come on, Marvin, boy!" He heard Jim's voice from the bench. "Hit it when it's in there!"

He ticked the next one. It went sailing back over the catcher's shoulder, striking the backstop screen.

"You're feeling it!" He heard Jim shout again.

He got ready for the third pitch. With two strikes on him and no balls, he was in a tough spot. His heart thumped against his ribs. He wished Jim had not put him second in the batting order. Everybody would expect too much from him. Down in eighth or ninth, or even seventh position, nobody expected you to hit every time you stepped to the plate.

The pitcher wound up, threw. Marvin put his left foot forward, lifted his bat. But the ball was coming in too wide. He let it go by.

"Ball!" said the umpire.

For a second his heart stood in his throat. Just suppose the umpire had yelled "Strike!"

Now the count was two to one. He felt a little better. The nervousness had partly left him. Again the pitcher wound up, threw the ball. It came in straight and a little low, but it looked as if it might be a strike. He swung.

Missed!

"Strike three!" cried the umpire.

Marvin dropped the bat and walked sadly back to the bench. He did not dare look up. He knew what everybody was thinking.

Jackie Barnes was up next. He hit the ball to the left of second base. Rick Savora followed him and hit the first one for a double. Everybody yelled. The next batter flied out, making it two outs. Then Chuck Sterns hit a grounder through short, scoring Jackie and Rick, and the next batter struck out.

When the Indians came to bat they scored three runs, and went ahead of the Tigers — 3 to 2.

II

IN the third inning, Marvin felt as nervous as he had the first time he had marched up to the plate. Larry Munson, their tall skinny pitcher, was up. He threw right-handed but batted left, something Marvin could not understand. He looked pretty gawky standing with his bat on his shoulder, his legs close together, and the brim of his blue cap bent through the middle like a triangle.

The Indians' pitcher threw a fast one down the center of the plate. Larry let it go, hardly lifting the bat from his shoulder. The next one looked as if it was heading for the same place. This time Larry shifted his right foot and brought his bat around in a hard swing. Crack! His bat met the ball and sent it sailing out to right field!

He ran to first, his long thin legs looking like something in a slow-motion picture, but Marvin could see he was covering ground fast. He circled first base, ran to second and stopped there, standing on the bag with both feet and his hands on his hips. The people roared.

Kenny Stokes, the lead-off man, was up again. He swung at the first ball. It dribbled in a slow grounder toward the pitcher, who fielded it and threw it easily to first.

Larry ran off second base a short distance, then ran back.

Marvin's turn came again. He walked to the plate, his feet feeling like lead weights. He had another bat this time, though he was sure it would not do any good.

"Come on, Marvin!" the boys on the bench yelled. "Bring Larry in! Bring him in!"

His heart was jumping. If he got a hit now probably Larry could make it home to tie the score. Everybody would forget his fanning out in that first inning. He dug his sneakers into the soft dirt — boys in the Grasshoppers League were not supposed to wear cleated shoes — and waited for the pitch.

It came in a little high, but it didn't look bad. Marvin cut at it. He heard a *crack!* as the bat met the ball. A blooper that looked as big as a balloon floated through the air toward the pitcher! Marvin threw down the bat, and started running slowly toward first.

"Run, Marvin!" he heard Jim shout. "Run!"

But the ball dropped into the pitcher's hands. Sadly, Marvin turned and headed back for the bench.

Nobody said anything to him, but he saw Rick suddenly rise from the bench and go toward Jim Cassell. Rick said something to Jim, then Jim turned and spoke to another boy on the bench.

"Artie, play catch with somebody," Marvin heard him say. "You're going in in place of Marvin next inning." He looked up at Marvin. "Marvin — "

"I heard you, Jim," Marvin said. As Rick started back toward his seat on the bench he came face to face with Marvin. Marvin's eyes hardened. His cheeks grew red.

"If you'd give my bat back to me," he said angrily, "I could hit that ball! You're a thief, that's what you are! You stole my bat!"

12

RICK's face paled and his mouth opened as if he was going to say something. But Marvin was already running out along the left field foul line, his eyes to the ground, not looking right or left. He had to get away from here, just as fast as he could. Someone yelled after him — it sounded like Jim's voice — but he paid no attention to it. He found his glove in the outfield where he had dropped it, picked it up, and kept on running.

He wondered what Jeannie and his mother and father would say. Well — what could they say? They could see that he could not hit the ball. It wasn't any more than right that he was taken out.

He saw a fat, chubby-legged little boy run out into the street chasing after a blue-and-red rubber ball. He wasn't over three years old — a little towhead.

A car whizzed around the corner, its tires screaming on the pavement. Marvin stared at it and then at the little boy. Sudden terror took hold of him. The fat little boy wasn't paying any attention to the car!

Suddenly the loud cry of a woman reached Marvin's ears. "Gary! Gary, get back here! Watch that car!"

There was fear in her voice. Marvin saw her standing in the doorway, one hand clutching her apron, the other on her chest. "Gary!" she screamed again.

The little boy did not move. Realizing that the car would not be able to stop in time, Marvin dove out into the street and picked up the boy, snatching him out of the way.

The car's brakes were squealing. The tires left twin black marks on the street. Then it stopped, and a man looked out of the window, his face ghost-white.

"Boy!" he exclaimed. "That was close!"

"I'll say it was!" said Marvin, with a
shudder. The little boy started to cry
and Marvin carried him to his mother,

who was running toward them from the house. He saw that the back yard of the house faced his back yard.

"Thank you!" she said to Marvin. "Thank you so much!" Marvin saw her white face as she bent and picked up her little son.

A tall, brown-haired man ran out of the house then, followed by a freckle-faced boy who was a year or two younger than Marvin. The boy's shirt was torn, and his corduroy pants had a long rip in one knee. Shakily, the woman told her husband what had happened. The husband looked at Marvin gratefully.

"That was quick thinking, son," he

said. "You sure make us very happy, going after little Gary like that. Sometime I'll see that you get something for this."

Marvin smiled. "That's all right," he said. "I'm glad I came by when I did."

He went home, feeling happy at the man's words.

He had hardly been home five minutes when a soft knock sounded on the door. He knew it wasn't Daddy or Mother. They wouldn't knock.

Wondering, he went to the door and opened it. It was the freckle-faced boy whose little brother he had saved from the path of the car. He was holding a bat in his hand — lifting it up to Marvin.

Marvin's eyes went wide. It was his missing bat!

13

AT the ball field the next afternoon, just before practice, Marvin approached Rick. He had a lump in his throat.

"Rick, I — I'm sorry that I said you had my bat. I got it back yesterday. Freckles Ginty was the one who took it out of my yard."

Rick looked at him a moment before he said anything. Finally he shrugged his shoulders and said, "Okay. You got it back. Maybe you can hit that ball now."

Marvin felt the sarcasm in his voice. He wondered if he and Rick would ever be friends. He wished they would be. Rick was tough in a way, but everybody liked him. He usually wanted his way about things, but he was almost always right, too — and he was a good ball-player. Someday, Marvin thought, Rick might play in the big leagues.

"Did you go in their house?" Rick said suddenly. Marvin had started to turn away, but now that Rick spoke he turned back.

"No," he said. "But Mr. and Mrs. Ginty look like awfully nice people."

"They are. You should see some of

the things Mr. Ginty makes out of wood. Freckles showed me once."

"Nice?"

"Nice? Sometime have Freckles take you in his house. He'll show you!"

"I will!" smiled Marvin.

Thursday afternoon they had another Grasshoppers League game. It was with the Bears. Jim had Artie play instead of Marvin. Artie hit a slow roller the first time up, and was put out. In the field he missed a fly ball that scored a runner for the Bears.

"He can't catch or hit," Kenny Stokes said. "At least, Marv could catch that ball!"

Marvin felt pleased to hear Kenny say that. He was sitting on the bench,

holding the bat in his hand. His own
bat. He had told Jim that he had finally
gotten it back, trying to hint that now
he would be able to hit. But Jim had
only grinned and said that he was glad.

Marvin fidgeted on the bench. He
wished Jim would let him take Artie's
place. He felt sure he could hit now.

Then all at once Jim called to him.
"Okay, Marvin. Go out to left field!"

14

MARVIN dropped his bat under the bench, picked up his glove, and ran out to left field. A fly ball came out to him. He caught it easily.

When it was time to bat he wasn't nervous any more. The bat felt just right in his hand. He felt good. He waited for the pitcher's throw — and the very first pitch he hit for a single!

The crowd yelled. He could hear

Jim's voice — "Thataboy, Marv! I knew you could do it!"

Finally came the sixth inning, the important moment, with the score 8 to 6 in the Bears' favor. The bases were loaded. Marvin again was up to bat. A hit could tie the score. A good long drive could win the ball game. Many a time Marvin had thought of a moment like this, when he would come to the plate with three on. Now it had really happened.

Before he got into the box he rested his bat on the ground, reached down and rubbed some dirt into his palms to dry off the sweat. He had seen Barry do that. Then he picked up the bat and stepped into the box. The pitcher stepped onto the mound, looked at the runner on third, then lifted his arm and threw the ball toward the plate.

It was chest-high. It looked good to Marvin. He put his left foot forward and brought back his bat. He swung, and

the *crack!* sounded throughout the park as bat met ball.

Like a white bullet the ball shot over the shortstop's head. Marvin dropped the bat and scampered for first. The ball hit the grass halfway between the left fielder and the center fielder, who both ran as fast as they could after it. It bounced on beyond them!

One run scored! Two! Three! Marvin ran in from third. One of the fielders picked up the ball and heaved it in. But it was too late.

Marvin crossed the plate — a home run!

It won the game — 10 to 8.

15

THE bat was lucky, all right. Marvin kept on hitting the ball in every game. Jim placed him third in the batting order, just before Rick. At the end of their fifth game his batting average was .453 and Rick's .422. Barry Welton came to see Marvin play whenever he wasn't playing himself. Of course, Jeannie and his mother and daddy never missed a ball game.

Then one day Jim Cassell called Marvin aside. It was after they had won a game that put them in the lead five wins to one loss. Marvin held his bat and glove in his hands as he looked up at Jim. He felt very happy. He had made three hits today, and had walked once. A perfect day at the plate!

Jim said, "Marvin, I've some nice news for you. How would you like to appear on television tonight?"

Marvin's heart jumped. "On television?"

Jim grinned. "Jerry Walker's sports program. He called me up last night. Says he sees by the papers that you're hitting the ball like a major leaguer, and he would like to have you on his program. He would like to ask you a few questions, I suppose."

"Boy! If it's okay with my mother and daddy — I sure would!"

He was bursting with pride when he told the news to them in the car. Their faces brightened with happiness. Jeannie clapped her hands.

"Wait till I tell Annie and Grace!" she cried. "They've got TV sets!"

"Well, you haven't said if I could go," Marvin murmured anxiously.

"Of course you can!" Mother exclaimed, and she pulled out a small handkerchief and wiped her eyes. Daddy smiled big too, but he did not say much. He just gave Marvin a strong hug. Whenever he appreciated something Marvin or Jeannie did, that was what he would always do. Give them a strong hug.

"May I ask Barry to come with us?" Marvin said.

"Certainly," his daddy said then. "You tell Barry and we'll pick him up when we go."

He saw Barry and shouted to him. Barry came over and Marvin told him what his daddy had suggested.

"That would be swell!" smiled Barry.

That night Marvin appeared on Jerry Walker's program. Mother, Daddy, Jeannie and Barry sat in another room, watching through a huge plate-glass window. At first sight of the cameras and lights Marvin was a little frightened and nervous. But by the time the program started, and Jerry Walker talked to him, he felt better. Jerry asked him how long had he played ball? What was his batting average? What did his mother and father think of his playing baseball?

Finally Jerry mentioned his bat. "Jim Cassell tells me you have a bat you won't let anybody else use," he said. "You must think a lot of that bat, Marvin," he added, smiling.

"I sure do," Marvin answered. "It's my lucky bat."

16

WHEN August came, the Tigers and the Bears were tied for first place. The boys were growing more excited by the day. They kept talking about the World Series game. Jim Cassell told them not to let the excitement of it make them forget about playing good baseball. But Marvin and the rest could see that Jim was pretty excited, himself.

"We've three more games to play,"

Jim said. "We must win two out of those three. If we win, we're in!"

They started playing the first of the three games. For the first two innings neither team scored. Then the Bears got on by a bunted ball that caught the Tigers off guard. It must have worried the Tiger pitcher, Larry Munson, because he walked the next man. The third batter hit a single that scored one run. The next batter hit a double to make the score 2 to 0.

A fly went out to left field that Marvin caught easily. The next hitter banged a liner toward Billy Weston at third, who caught it and threw it to second. The runner on second had started to run, thinking it was going for

a hit. He didn't get back in time. The second baseman touched the base and the runner was out.

In the fourth inning the Tigers scored two runs to even it up. It stayed that way till the first half of the sixth. Larry was first batter and got a single, a nice one over first base. Kenny Stokes walked. Then Marvin came up, and everybody cheered.

He swung at the first pitch. Missed! The next one was a ball. The third was in there. He swung hard and hit it — a neat single — but something terrible happened.

The bat broke in two! One piece he had in his hand. The other was flying out across the ground toward third base!

17

MARVIN did not know what to do. Without his bat he was sure everything would be the way it was before. He would not be able to hit again, and Jim would take him out of the game.

There were only two games left to play. The Tigers had won one. They must win one more. If they lost the next two games their chance of seeing a World Series game was gone.

It was a cloudy day. Marvin stayed

inside the house most of the time. He did not feel like going out. He did not feel like doing anything. He wished the baseball season were all over so that there would not be any more ball games. With his bat broken he might

as well quit playing. He would not go out on the ball field now. He knew he could not hit with any other bat. He just knew it.

"It isn't the bat, son," his daddy said to him. "It's you. You've got it in your head that you can't hit with any other bat, and you're wrong."

"But it's true, Daddy!" Marvin cried. "I can't hit with any other bat! I never could! Didn't I try it before?"

His father put a hand on his shoulder, and looked him squarely in the eye. "Look, Marvin," he said softly, "why do you think you can't hit with another bat, and still you were able to hit with the one Barry gave you?"

Marvin shrugged. "I don't know,

Daddy. Maybe there was something about that bat."

His daddy grinned. "Something lucky?"

He shrugged again. "I don't know. Maybe."

"You believe that *bat* was lucky?"

Marvin turned away. He wished his daddy would not talk about it any more. There was no use talking about it.

"I don't know, Daddy. I just know that every time I used that bat I'd hit the ball. I didn't always get a safety, but I'd hit it some place. I never did it with any other bat I used. Never!"

"Just try again," his daddy said. "Just try again, Marvin."

Marvin wished that it would rain on

Friday, the day of their next game.

In the morning it looked as if it was going to rain. But in the afternoon the clouds cleared away and the sun came out bright and hot. Jim still had Marvin bat third. Jim had no idea that a bat made a difference. He was like Daddy.

The first two men up flied out. When Marvin came to the plate he let the first pitch go. It was a strike. He let the next one go. That was a ball. He ticked the third pitch, which made the count two and one. His heart beat faster. From the bench he could hear Jim and Rick yelling:

"Hit it, Marvin! Hit it, boy!"

The fourth pitch came in. He swung — and struck out.

18

MARVIN dropped the bat and ran to the bench after his glove.

"Never mind that, Marv," Jim said. "You'll hit it the next time."

Marvin didn't say anything. When the next time came he would strike out again. Jim would find that out himself. Maybe he didn't believe the bat made a difference, but it did with Marvin. There must have been something about that bat. Striking out his first time up with another bat proved it. How could anybody say it didn't?

He caught a high fly ball that inning. The crowd cheered loudly, but it did not make him feel any happier.

When the Tigers came to bat again he did not have a chance to hit. The Bears' pitcher was too good. He threw hooks that fooled the Tiger hitters. Even Rick struck out.

Marvin trotted back out to the field. That first inning had surely gone fast. The first Bears' hitter stood at the plate and hardly took the bat off his shoulder. Larry was wild with him. Maybe it was because the batter was so small. Larry walked him.

The next batter hit a ground ball that

Kenny missed at short. It rolled to the outfield. Marvin and the center fielder dashed after it. Marvin picked it up and threw it to third. Now there was a man on first and second. Marvin returned to his position in left field and wished no more balls would come out to him.

Crack!

Larry's first pitch was hit for a long fly. It was coming Marvin's way! Marvin got his eye on it and watched it sail into the blue sky. He stepped back a little, then forward, then back again. The ball seemed to be zigzagging. Then suddenly it was curving downward. It was falling fast — dizzily. Marvin put up his gloved hand.

The ball hit the heel of his glove —
and dropped to the ground!

A roar burst from the crowd, died
quickly. Marvin bent, picked up the
ball, and heaved it to the infield. A run-

ner was tearing for home. Another was already on second. The shortstop got the ball and threw it home, but the runner had already scored. The man on second raced to third. The catcher saw him and whipped the ball to third. It sailed over the third baseman's head to the outfield. Marvin went after it. He took his time. He saw that the runner on third was already halfway home.

Three runs! Three runs because he had missed that fly ball! A lump formed in his chest, and grew into a big knot.

The game ended 7 to 4 in the Bears' favor.

19

ONE o'clock Saturday afternoon, and Marvin was still home. The game was scheduled to start at exactly one-thirty. He used to get there at twelve-thirty, or even a few minutes before. Today he did not care. Today he did not want to go at all. He had lost the ball game for the Tigers yesterday by missing that fly ball. He had struck out twice. Sure, he had hit the ball twice, too. But they were grounders, right into somebody's hands. They were not hits.

Not the kind he used to get with his own bat.

That bat was lucky. No matter what Daddy, or Jim, or anybody said. He had never been as good as people said he was. The credit belonged to the bat. Nobody had known that but Marvin. Maybe now they'd find out where the credit had really belonged!

His daddy appeared at the living room door. A frown crossed his forehead, as if he was surprised to see Marvin sitting there.

"Marvin! I thought you had gone to the field?"

Marvin met his eyes, then looked away. His heart started to pound. "I'm not going to the game," he said.

"Why not?"

"Because I'm no good. I can't hit. I can't field. Jim just lets me play because I used to be good."

"That's no way to talk, son," his daddy said, smiling. "Jim lets you play because he knows you're good. You're just thinking about that bat again. And you're wrong. I wish I could make you understand that."

The doorbell chime clanged and his daddy went to answer it. Marvin heard a familiar voice ask for him.

"Marvin!" his daddy called. "Someone to see you!"

Marvin got off the chair. He walked across the room to the door, and stopped. It was Freckles Ginty.

He smiled so that the freckles on his face were almost crawling over each other.

"Hello, Marvin," he smiled. "I got something for you."

Marvin frowned. "What?"

"This!"

From behind his back Freckles pulled a bat. Marvin stared. It was exactly like the one he had broken!

His mouth fell open. For a moment he could not speak. Then he managed to say: "Where — where did you get it?"

"It's the same one you broke," Freckles said, grinning. "My father fixed it together again for you."

20

STRIKE one!" yelled the umpire. Marvin drew his foot back and rested the bat again on his shoulder. He wasn't worried about having a strike called on him. This was his fourth trip to the plate. Outside of hitting a long fly ball that the center fielder had caught in the third inning, he had two hits. One was a single, the other a triple.

Mr. Ginty had sure paid Marvin back

for saving his little boy on the street that day. Imagine fixing up the bat so that it was like new again! He sure was a wonderful man!

The pitcher threw in another one. "Ball!" said the umpire. "One and one!"

The score was 7 to 5. The Tigers were ahead. There was a man on first. It would not hurt to knock in another run. The Bears were good players. You could not tell when they might start hitting Larry hard and threaten to win the ball game. The team that won this game won the trip to the World Series.

"Come on, Marv!" the gang on the bench shouted. "Come on, kid! Hit that apple!"

Then he heard his daddy. "Come on, Marv! Drive it!"

He felt his heart swell inside him. He seldom heard his daddy shout at the ball games.

Suddenly the pitch came in. He stepped into it and lifted the bat.

He swung. *Crack!* The bat met the ball and it sailed out between left and center fields! He dropped the bat and ran. He touched first, then second, then third — and he did not stop until he crossed home plate!

A home run!

"Hurray! Marv!" everybody roared.

Rick caught him and shook his hand. "Thataboy, Marv! Thataboy!"

"Nice going, Marv!" exclaimed Jim.

"Guess we'll be heading for the World Series game!"

Marvin grinned. His heart beat so fast from running and from happiness he thought it would leap right out of his shirt.

The Bears lost hope after Marvin's long clout. They didn't score any more runs. The Tigers won — 9 to 5.

Jeannie ran to her brother right after the game and hugged him. Then came his daddy and mother. Then Barry Welton.

"You'll be a big leaguer one of these days, Marvin," Barry smiled.

Marvin returned the smile, then shook his head. "I can't use this bat all my life," he said, holding up the bat. "It'll be too small when I grow up."

Another voice broke in, a soft voice Marvin had heard only once before. "Marvin, I have a confession to make. I hope you'll forgive me if I tell you."

Marvin looked around. It was Mr.

Ginty, Freckles's father. Marvin was puzzled. "What do you mean, Mr. Ginty?" he said.

Mr. Ginty smiled. "I made that bat, Marvin."

Marvin stared. His heart flew to his throat. "You — you mean it isn't the one I used to have? The one that Barry gave me? The one I busted in two?"

"No. It isn't. I don't think I could ever fix that other one up so that you could use it again. This is a brand-new bat. I made it myself — just for you."

Marvin swallowed hard. He put out his hand. Mr. Ginty took it. "Thanks, Mr. Ginty! Thanks — a lot!" Marvin cried.

Then he turned to his daddy. He

could barely see him through the tears that blurred his eyes. His daddy smiled back.

"You see? It wasn't the bat, was it, son?" he said.

Marvin shook his head.

It was himself, all right.